This Book Belongs to:

Mickey's Young Readers Library

VOLUME
8

Tigger and the Apple Tree

STORY BY MARY CAREY

Activities by Thoburn Educational Enterprises, Inc.

A BANTAM BOOK
NEW YORK · TORONTO · LONDON · SYDNEY · AUCKLAND

Tigger and the Apple Tree   A Bantam Book/September 1990. All rights reserved. © 1990 The Walt Disney Company. Developed by The Walt Disney Company in conjunction with Nancy Hall, Inc. This book may not be reproduced or transmitted in any form or by any means.

ISBN 0–553–05623–9

Published simultaneously in the United States and Canada. Bantam Books are published by Bantam Doubleday Dell Publishing Group, Inc. Its trademark, consisting of the words "Bantam Books" and the portrayal of a rooster, is Registered in U.S. Patent and Trademark Office and in other countries. Marca Registrada. Bantam Books 666 Fifth Avenue, New York, New York 10103.

Printed in the United States of America

0 9 8 7 6 5 4 3 2 1

A Walt Disney BOOK FOR YOUNG READERS

It was a bright fall morning—the sort of morning
Winnie the Pooh liked best. He sat on his doorstep
in the warm sunshine and hummed a little tune.
    Suddenly Pooh saw Rabbit trotting along the
path. Rabbit was carrying a basket. He looked
worried and hurried.

Pooh stopped his humming. "Good morning, Rabbit," he said. "Where are you going in such a hurry? And why are you carrying that basket?"

"Good morning, Pooh Bear," said Rabbit. "This is my apple-picking basket. The apples on the tree down the path are nice and ripe, and I am going to pick them. Then I'll make my special applesauce with honey for my young cousins. They are coming to visit today."

Pooh thought about applesauce. He was very fond of applesauce—especially applesauce with honey in it.

"Let me help you," said Pooh. He hurried along with Rabbit.

When they got to the apple tree, Pooh and
Rabbit began to pick the apples. It was easy to
reach the ones on the lower branches. Soon the two
friends had picked almost all of them. That is when
Pooh began to wonder and worry.

"How many apples do we need?" he asked
Rabbit.

"A basketful," said Rabbit. "My grandma's recipe starts out, 'Take one basket of apples . . .'"

With that, Rabbit jumped up and picked the last ripe apple on the last low branch.

"Rabbit, we have a problem," said Pooh. "The basket is still mostly empty."

"We must pick the apples from the high
branches if we want to fill the basket," said Pooh.
"One of us will have to climb the tree."

Just as Pooh said this, Roo came hopping by. He
was in time to hear Rabbit say, "Climb the tree? Oh,
would you, Pooh? That's very good of you."

"Can you climb that big tree, Pooh?" squeaked
Roo. "Can you?"

Tigger bounced across the meadow then. He was singing about the wonderful things tiggers do. Then he saw Pooh and Rabbit and Roo. He stopped bouncing, and he stopped singing.

Pooh looked up at the apple tree. "Did I really
say I would climb that very high tree?" he asked.
"You did, Pooh," cried Roo. "You said that."
Roo turned to Tigger. "He said that, Tigger. Pooh
is going to climb to the top and pick all the apples!"

"Climb that little tree?" said Tigger. "Why, that's nothing. Just watch the way a tigger gets to the top!"

"You mean *you'll* climb the tree, Tigger?" asked Pooh. He looked very happy to hear this.

"Oh, I won't climb," said Tigger. "I'll bounce up there. It's what tiggers do."

"Don't listen to him, Pooh," said Rabbit. "You know how Tigger brags. You know how he starts things and doesn't finish them."

Pooh heard what Rabbit had said. And he did warn Tigger not to forget to pick the apples while he was bouncing.

"Don't forget, Tigger. Rabbit needs the apples to make applesauce with honey," Pooh said.

"Don't be silly. Tiggers never forget," Tigger said. He bounced a big bounce and picked an apple. Roo cheered, and Pooh looked even happier.

"We're going to be sorry, Pooh Bear," warned Rabbit. "Tigger will ruin things somehow. He always does."

"Not always," said Pooh. "Besides, someone has to pick the high apples. Otherwise you won't have enough apples to make applesauce."

"All right, all right," said Rabbit. "But you know what a show-off Tigger is. Remember what happened with the bee tree."

"What happened?" asked Roo.

"Tigger was trying to get a pawful of honey in one bounce," Rabbit explained. "He got stuck in the tree. And the bees got upset. And then the bees started heading for me!"

"That just shows that bees are not very smart," said Tigger. He bounced again. And Roo laughed.

Kanga came along just then. "Roo, dear, not so loud. You'll wake Owl."

"I'm awake," said a low, grumpy voice.
It was Owl. He flew to sit on the fence near the apple tree. He rubbed the sleep from his eyes.
Tigger did a backward somersault in the air.
"My word!" said Owl. "Isn't Tigger remarkable!"

"Tiggers *are* remarkable!" laughed Tigger.
He bounced onto Owl's front porch and rang Owl's doorbell, even though he knew Owl was not at home.

"I knew it!" cried Rabbit. "Didn't I tell you? He doesn't care about apples. He just wants to show off!"

Just then Piglet came running up the path.
"What's all the shouting about?" asked Piglet.
"It's about tiggers," called Tigger. "Look at me!"
He bounced into the air and did *two* backward
somersaults.

Eeyore had come along in time to see Tigger's tricks.

"That's wonderful," said Eeyore. "If that's the sort of thing that makes you happy."

"It would make *me* happy if Tigger would pick those apples," complained Rabbit.

So Tigger bounced again. This time he picked an apple with his toes.

He dropped the apple into Rabbit's basket.
Suddenly Rabbit felt hopeful. Perhaps for once
Tigger would finish what he began. Perhaps he
would pick all the apples like a sensible animal.

But Tigger was not a sensible animal. He could not just pick apples. He had to pick apples without looking. He had to pick apples while he did somersaults. He had to pick apples with his back to the tree.

Every time he picked an apple, Piglet shouted "Hooray!"

Roo cried, "Higher, Tigger. Bounce higher!"

"Be careful, Tigger," said Rabbit. "You'll get hurt. You'll smash the apples, too."

"Look, Rabbit, there are only two apples left at the top of the tree. If Tigger can pick those, your basket will be full," said Pooh.

"What do you mean, *if* I can pick them?" said Tigger. "I can't miss. I can do it with my eyes shut!"

"Oh, no, Tigger!" cried Rabbit. "Not with your eyes shut! Watch what you're doing, Tigger!"

But Tigger did not listen. He leaped onto a fence and balanced there. He closed his eyes. Then he bounced.

It was a wonderful bounce. Up Tigger flew. Higher! Higher!

Up he flew to the very top of the apple tree. He landed on a slender, swaying branch that bent under his weight.

At first Tigger did not feel the bending and the swaying. He picked the last two apples. He tossed them down to Pooh.

Tigger watched the apples drop. They fell and
fell. Suddenly Tigger saw how high up he was.
Suddenly he felt the branch bending under him.
  He held tight to the tree and didn't move.
  "Come down, Tigger," called Piglet. "The basket
is full."

Tigger could not come down. He could not let go of that tree. "I didn't know it was so high when I bounced up here," he wailed.

"That's what comes of not watching what you're doing," scolded Rabbit. "If you would look before you bounce, you'd see how high things are."

"Take your time," said Eeyore. He was trying to be of help. "Climb down slowly."

"I can't," moaned Tigger. "If I climb, I could slip. If I slip, I might fall. Slipping and falling are not what tiggers do best."

Suddenly there was a horrid cracking noise.
"Oh, no!" cried Tigger. "It's breaking!"
"Bounce down, Tigger!" called Pooh. "It's the
way you got up there."
"I can't!" cried Tigger. "When I see how far
down it is, I get dizzy!"
"Then shut your eyes so you can't see," said
Pooh.

The branch cracked again.

"Hurry!" shouted Pooh.

Tigger squeezed his eyes shut. He counted,
"One! Two! Three!" Then he bounced off the
branch.

"I can't look!" moaned Rabbit.

Down came Tigger—down, down, down!
    He landed right in Rabbit's basket. He made a
wet, splashy sort of sound, but he wasn't hurt in the
least. Roo and Piglet cheered.
    "There!" said Pooh. "I knew you could do it!"

Rabbit opened his eyes. He saw Tigger climb out of the basket. Tigger had bits of apple all over him. "My apples!" cried Rabbit. "You smashed my apples. And there are no more in the Hundred-Acre Wood. My young cousins will be here soon, and I'll have no applesauce with honey for them!"

Kanga smiled. "No harm done, Rabbit," she said gently. "In fact, Tigger has done half of your work for you."

"Done half of my work?" echoed Rabbit. "He's squashed all my apples, that's what he's done."

"Exactly," said Kanga. "You'd have to do that yourself to make applesauce, wouldn't you?"

"Your applesauce will be just fine," said Pooh. "I have extra honey at home. Would you like it? I'll run and get it for you."

Rabbit blinked. Then he began to smile. "Why, thank you very much, Pooh Bear," he said. "Thank you, Kanga. And Tigger . . . thank you, Tigger."

Rabbit took the apples home and made his applesauce with honey.

Pooh helped. He brought extra honey, and he tasted to make sure the applesauce was just right.

When Rabbit's young cousins arrived, Rabbit had everything ready for them. He had everything ready for his friends, too. He couldn't have made the applesauce without them.

Everyone ate two dishes of applesauce with honey. Some ate three because it tasted so good.

Everyone cheered for Rabbit because he made the applesauce. And everyone cheered for Tigger because he had picked the apples. Tigger bounced a big bounce to show Rabbit's young cousins how he did it. "But from now on," he said, with a great big wink for Rabbit, "I'll keep my eyes open when I bounce!"

Think About It

Let's Talk!

Think about these questions. Then retell the story in your own words.

Near what kind of tree does the story take place?
Why did Rabbit need the apples from the tree?
Who was there?
Why did Tigger bounce?
What did Tigger learn?

What's Wrong
With This Picture?

Point to the four things that do not belong in the
story of Tigger and the Apple Tree.

Fun With Words

What's Going On?

Look at the pictures in the story below. Can you figure out what's going on?

One day, met Rabbit, who was on his way to the apple tree to pick . Pooh went along with  and they picked as many apples as they could from the . But they couldn't reach the high up in the tree. Along came who offered to bounce up the to get the . Tigger bounced up, down, and all around until all the , even the very highest, were picked. But 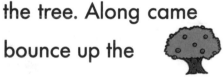 got stuck in the tree, and when he finally bounced down, he landed in Rabbit's ! Then  made honey-applesauce from all the squashed , and everyone enjoyed it.

Which Ones Can Do The Same Things?

1. Which ones can fly?

2. Which ones can laugh?

3. Which ones can run?

4. Which ones can bounce?

Young Readers Library • Mickey's Young Readers Library • Mickey's
Readers Library • Mickey's Young Readers Library • Mickey's Young
Mickey's Young Readers Library • Mickey